The Langham first opened its doors to
1913, and has been a landmark on
Bought originally by two wealthy sist
Martyr, the hotel remained in their family for 92 years. Charlotte's great-grandson, Julian Martyr, ran the Langham for 23 years until 2005, when it was purchased by the present owners Wendy and Neil Kirby. With an original Belisha beacon and zebra crossing immediately outside, the hotel is at a strategic point on the promenade as the crossing brings people directly towards the Langham. It was one of the key features that encouraged the Kirbys to buy the hotel. Once seven Victorian houses, the 80 bedroom hotel still retains many of its original features and has an elegant period style combined with the modern technology and comforts demanded by twenty-first century guests. The Langham has won many awards and in 2013 it became the first and only AA-four star hotel in Eastbourne.

Langham Hotel, 43-49 Royal Parade, Eastbourne BN22 7AH

Tel: 01323 731451   email: frontdesk@langhamhotel.co.uk

website: www.langhamhotel.co.uk

Best Wishes

Gregory Gorrel

The Christmas Tree Story

Published by Mithra Publishing in 2017
www.mithrapublishing.com

About the author

Gregory Gower was born in 1935 – so growing up and schooling were mixed with a world in turmoil. Most persons have the luxury of not experiencing bombs being dropped on them. He was four years of age when the war started and ten when it ended. Many days and nights were spent in an air raid shelter having to cope with listening to a gun emplacement nearby firing at enemy aircraft who were dropping their deadly cargo over Kent.

A noise so loud you would have thought your ears would have burst. His house had a direct hit and he was still in bed fast asleep when the curtains and the foot of his bed caught alight and he was rescued by a A.R.P. Warden! Many houses were destroyed and damaged later when the first of the many doodlebugs dived into the road.

He managed to gain his 11 plus at the age of 13. He went to Westwood Secondary Modern School then onto Dartford Grammar School.

First job was training as a Compositor in Posners, Walters and Harrisons, Shoe Lane, Fleet Street. Second job was with Jones and Darke Rubber Plantation Office in Fenchurch Street.

He joined the Royal Air Force in 1953. Was sent abroad and served in Aden where experienced active service. Five months later he was posted to a Fighter Station/Staging Post at Sharjah where he served out the remainder of his service.

On leaving the Royal Air Force, he became a Civil Servant and worked in the Passport Office and then transferred to 13 Downing Street in the United Nations Department.

Became seriously ill in 1960 and ended up in the Neurological Ward at Brooke Hospital – not expected to live!

In 1976 met Brenda and after a short engagement, married her in 1977. They have one Ginger cat called Josie who brings in leaves and feathers, but no mice – yet!

He is an acting/singing member and Vice Chairman of Eastbourne Gilbert and Sullivan Society. He is editor for NODA National Operatic & Dramatic Association News Magazine for South East England.

A columnist for an on-line Newspaper – thesussexnewspaper.com. A collection Secretary for N.C.H. Action for Children Charity in Eastbourne and is a member of Eastbourne Central Methodist Church Choir.

Visit www.bookworm.org.uk

Other books by the same author:

Picture Poetry Painting Book

Derbyshire Reflections & Others) Poetry, Prose

With Mixed Feelings) & Goodness Knows

Food For Thought   Poetry, Prose & Recipes

A Touch of Heaven & Other Short Stories

I Remember it Well & other Short Stories

Christmas is Coming Short Stories & Sketches

Mistaken Identity

A Joyride to Murder & The Steal

The Adventures of Bertram Bear with Illustrations by Amanda Breach

In the Pipeline

A Sequel to Murder

TIME A Sci-fi with three endings

Bertram Bear and the Rivals

Bertram Bear Rules

Bertram Bear and the Ginger Cat

Bertram Bear on Holiday

Bertram Bear in Pantomime

The Treasure

It Can Happen in a Week

Future projects

Rhyme & Reason Poetry & Prose - some new, some old

Letters to Nobody

Hidden Agenda

Stranglehold

Enigma

Inspector Graves Investigates

Bertram Bear's World

Bertram Bear and the Burglars

Bertram Bear Goes Back in Time

Bertram Bear Visits the Toy Shop

Bertram Bear Finds Buried Treasure

Bertram Bear Goes Hunting

Living With Hope or Call Me Madam! - Autobiography

About Amanda Breach

Amanda Breach is an Illustrator based in Eastbourne, East Sussex.

She achieved a BA Honours degree in Illustration at Middlesex university in London and now works as a freelance illustrator. Amanda works in a variety of media for her work including traditional watercolour painting, pencil work and digital art. She has worked on a variety of Projects ranging from children's illustrated books to stationary, shop fronts and advertising. Amanda enjoys working from her home and garden where she has created a unique range of Little Fox greeting cards. In Amanda's spare time she loves to take her sketchbook around with her and draw at different locations.

You can find out more about Amanda and see more of her work on her website www.amandabreachillustrations.co.uk

The Christmas Tree Story

The Christmas Tree Story

PROLOGUE

Children of all ages whether they be the adult variety or the very small, will never see Father Christmas because his magic would not work should any animal or human being be present at the time of his arrival on earth.

He visits each dwelling on earth in the hope that he can spread peace, happiness and hope for a better world and that each family receives the blessings of Christmastide, the dust of joy, the sky of laughter.

The night before Christmas Day is a bewitching time when some things remain unexplained and mingled with the stillness of the night are muffled sounds that remain a secret.

To those who believe in the true spirit of Christmas, it will all be straightforward.

Now to our special Christmas story which holds some of the magic that has been written about. It will be in your own favour if you remember this prologue which holds some of the vital clues to help you understand more fully what is about to unfold.

The time: The Present Day   *Setting: An Edwardian House*

An old fashioned family who believe in a truly traditional Christmas.

The Christmas Tree Story

A Christmas tree stood in the corner, the branches spreading in layers from top to bottom and festooned on each branch were fairy lights, tinsel, berries and beads of various sizes and colour. He was a very proud and noble tree having grown up in Kings Meadow, a well established Tree Farm.

He had been a very small sapling of five inches and now had grown to a modest 6' 6." He was a perfect specimen. Very symmetrical! At the very top was the prettiest fairy he had ever seen (let's be honest, he hadn't seen a fairy before). She was dressed in white flowing robes of finest silk and satin and her wings were thin and transparent.

The Christmas tree was also the guardian of many presents and even more so, he was the guardian of the house for the whole family were out carol singing. Christmas tree yawned noisily and stretched out his middle two branches and rubbed his eyes as he looked around the darkened room and said, 'It's about time we had some lights.'

He looked up at the Fairy, and as he was in charge he thought he would exert some authority in his voice and said, 'Fairy, Put the lights on please.'

(He was always told to say please after every question he asked as it went a long way to getting things done and besides it was always polite protocol, you know.) Lo and behold the Christmas tree lights shone so brightly which made the whole room come alive and the tree placed the two unadorned branches on his hips and bending forwards and backwards with joy, he smiled with glee to see his lower branches twinkling red, blue, purple, pink, green and white.

'Oh! This is absolutely beautiful!' he shouted with excitement.

He bent further forward and he saw all the presents beneath him, and then he bent backwards and he could see that the presents went all the way round his big tub where his roots were planted. He was beside himself with anticipation and he felt rather good at this moment in time. Christmas Tree looked around the room. It was festooned with decorations galore. He noticed the large patterned wall-paper which was well suited as the room was quite large. He had been told that rooms like this still existed and if he was lucky enough, he could very well be in one to take pride of place and be in charge.

Christmas Tree said to Fairy and to anyone else who was listening that from now on he would be known as CT as it sounded more friendly.

He had an idea that it would be good to stretch his limbs even further and he was thinking about his roots. However, he failed to notice how shiny the wooden floor was.

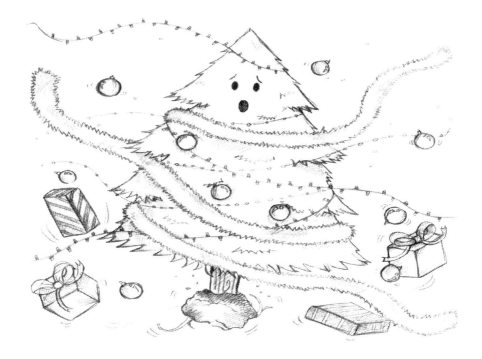

CT decided that this would be a good time to test his roots by taking them out of the tub and with great strength he began to pull one root up and placed it carefully on the floor. He then pulled his other root out and placed it down and immediately slipped across the floor scattering the presents everywhere. He stopped just short of the Grandfather clock who boomed out the eight o'clock chimes!

'That was not very clever young man! You almost damaged my case with your dirty great roots and they are extremely muddy! Should you be out of your tub?'

CT looked up at the clock and said rather feebly, 'Help.'

'I can't help you, I'm just a clock and I tick tock all day, chime the time and quite frankly I find it rather boring! Tick-tock tick-tock tick-tock! You see, don't you think that's boring?'

'I don't think so, said CT. 'At least you are here all the time! I only last over the Christmas period, after that I'm a goner.'

'Not necessarily so.' chimed the Clock.

'Isn't it?' said CT.

Clock said, 'If you keep your needles intact and you don't go brown, they may plant you in their garden! But look at you, your Fairy is lopsided, your fairy-lights have gone out and the tinsel is screwed up and the threads holding your beads have all broken! You will need a miracle to get yourself sorted!' Tree looked decidedly crestfallen.

'What should he do?' He thought Fairy might help. He looked down and saw she was straightening her tiara, taking the creases out of her wings, one of which was rather badly bent and brushing down her white silky robes. The star had come off her wand and you know if fairies lose a star it would mean having to order another one and that would mean filling in forms as to how it came off and goodness knows what, and she wouldn't be able to do any magic and would have to return to her depot to await further orders and probably allocated to do something quite awful which would mean filling out some more forms and so forth.

CT said, 'Fairy! Can you help me get up?'

Fairy said, 'Without my star, I am unable to do anything and it would have been nice had you said sorry, I mean to say I have to be on parade tomorrow morning when my Commander-in-chief, the Fairy Queen, comes round to inspect to see if everything is okay and look at me. What a mess! Find my star and I'll try and help you.'

CT and Clock looked round the room and saw a mouse struggling with a very bright object which happened to be the star they were looking for. Both CT and Clock boomed out. 'Mouse, Where are you taking that star?' The startled mouse looked round and boldly said. 'It's going on my wall, it will light up my home and make a nice decoration too!' Clock and CT said simultaneously, 'You can't do that!' 'Why!' said Mouse. 'Because you can't!' said Fairy striding across the room where mouse stood holding the star behind his back, which was so bright that Fairy had to put on her special dark glasses which she had in a bag concealed about her person.

All fairies had this added extra for such occasions as this, because it is known in the Fairy World that as soon as a star becomes detached it becomes brighter, so that it is easily spotted. Fairy prodded Mouse with her wand. 'Please place my star on my wand!' Mouse said, 'Shan't!' Fairy said again, 'Please, please place my star on my wand!' Mouse said, 'Why should I, I found it, finders keepers!' Fairy said. 'You can't have it, it is the property of Stars R Us Company and are loaned out to all fairies at Christmas time and other special occasions such as tooth time and besides I shall get demoted to third grade if I lose this star, because I have already mislaid two. I shall be made human for the Pantomime season and end up with Cinderella, and who in their right mind wants to do that!'

'Oh yes you do!' said Mouse. 'Oh no I don't!' said Fairy.

It was with some reluctance that mouse saw the reasoning behind it all, especially once having placed the star back on the wand, the good fairy waved her wand and Mouse's home lit up and was filled with lots of decorations and presents galore. Mouse ran into the house and tripped over one of the parcels. He picked himself up and looked around his room and yelled, 'Oh boy!' He went outside and thanked Fairy and wished her, CT and Clock A Happy Christmas and disappeared once more into his brightly lit home.

Mouse shouted out, 'I'm home darling – how's your day been?' Mrs. Mouse came out of the kitchen and said, 'Where have all these presents come from, I hope you haven't been spending your pay packet on useless gifts again – we have a budget to keep to and where's that light coming from?' Mr Mouse said, 'I met a fairy!' Mrs. Mouse said, 'A likely story – you've been dipping into our joint account again – I told you we can't afford luxuries like this – I just don't know what's wrong with you – you don't listen to a word I say!' Mr Mouse said, 'Have you quite finished? I met a fairy, honest!' Mr and Mrs Mouse went into a huddle and we slowly move away from their argument and see what's going on with CT, Fairy and Clock.

Fairy strode back to CT who had his head bowed down in regret, feeling sorry for himself. 'How could I have done such a reckless thing trying to walk across a floor with no feet?' Clock did two separate jingles. 'It is now eight thirty!' Clock liked to tell everybody the time, he couldn't tell anyone during the day. It wasn't protocol.

Fairy's tiara kept sliding to one side with every step she took and it was understandable that it annoyed her immensely and that's why CT kept getting menacing looks from her. 'Now CT! Let me see! I shall probably be able to get you back into your tub – but that's all, my powers are limited!' Fairy still had her dark glasses on, which was a good thing and she waved her wand. There was a blinding flash and a sizzling noise and hey presto CT was back in his tub.

The tree lights were not working – the tinsel was still screwed up and the beads and presents were still scattered to the four corners of the room and the most damaging thing of all was the unexplained muddy skid mark across the floor. CT sighed in dismay. 'This is the end – I'm done for! Look at me, what a terrible mess, if the family come into the room………..' CT's words trailed off as they all heard the front door opening and many excited voices could be heard and one clear voice rang out. 'Can I look at the tree again, Father?' 'Oh let us look!' the others said. 'No!' said Father, 'Let's leave it alone for tonight as Father Christmas will be coming down the chimney and we don't want to disturb the room.'

At that moment the clock struck nine o'clock. The noise seemed deafening and CT put one of branches up to his lips and said 'SSSHHUSS!' But clock went on – 'It's nine o'clock and that's me finished for the night until tomorrow morning – union rules and besides I need my shuteye – you will only hear my heart beating tick-tock – tick-tock – tick-tock! Good night Fairy! Good night CT!' CT cried, 'Don't leave me alone, I need someone to talk to and reassure me that everything will be alright in the morning!'

Clock looked around the room and said, 'You must be joking – look at the mess!' Clock said, 'I really do need to rest, when you've been on the go all day from nine am to nine pm – that's an awful lot of chiming!' Clock closed his eyes. Fairy flew to one of CT's lower branches and straightened her tiara again mumbling 'if only I had two hair clips'.

Then something happened that wasn't on anyone's agenda. A cat had pushed open the door and went straight to Mr and Mrs Mouse's door. The cat could not understand why there was a light coming from the skirting board. He placed one eye up to their door and Mr and Mrs Mouse were dancing. Round and round they went. Cat moved back on his haunches and said, 'This is really cool! They must be having a party. I wonder if I could be their surprise guest?' he said, licking his lips in anticipation.

'Oh no!' cried CT, 'What now – what do we do now?'

Fairy answered, 'Let's see what happens!'

Clock was snoring very loudly at this point and his snore woke him up. 'What's up?'

Fairy said, 'Look! It's the cat, he's by the mouse hole!'

'Oh goodness me,' said Clock. Last time he was here he did something unmentionable behind my casing, I can't go into details – it's too painful.'

Cat placed his eye up to the hole again and Mr and Mrs Mouse on seeing the cat stopped dancing and clung to the back wall of their home which contained a living room with dining area, kitchen, two beds and the usual other places.

They saw this menacing one eye and when they recovered from their initial shock, they asked cat if he was from London! Cat was puzzled by the question and asked why. Mr Mouse said, 'We thought for one moment you were in the wrong fairy story!' Cat said, 'No! I live here in this big house and when did you two move in?' 'Quite recently!' said mouse. Cat remarked that he knew the previous tenant and that he was quite a nice fellow!

Fairy and CT whispered to each other. 'What do you think they are talking about?' CT beckoned Clock, 'What are they talking about?' Clock said, 'The cat's menu I think'

Fairy and CT looked at each other in horror.

CT said he couldn't go on and what a disaster, the worst evening in his life, although there hadn't been many of them as he had only been delivered the day before yesterday, whenever that was. Fairy remarked on CT's selfish view, keeping on about what a terrible mess everything is and had he not done this or that this may never had happened and Fairy slammed down her foot in a bit of a temper on one of his branches and a pain shot right up her leg. It was a prickly bit that she had stamped on. 'Sorry! Sorry! Sorry!' said CT looking down at the drama.

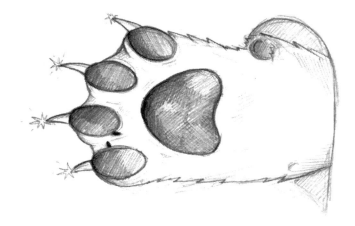

Cat decided action was needed and he pushed his paw through the hole and one by one his claws opened and each claw had a point which understandably frightened Mr and Mrs Mouse. Cat said, 'I won't hurt you, just flexing my paw you know.' Cat made sweeping motions but was unable to grab anything. Clock said, 'If you believe that you'll believe anything!' Cat looked at Clock and hissed and withdrew his paw from the hole and thought he would try a different ploy. 'I say Mrs Mouse. You have a nice home! Where did you get all this lovely furniture?' Mrs Mouse looked coy and said, 'Mr Mouse made it from chippings and compressed the material with dirt' 'She's knowledgeable,' said Clock. As cat spoke Mr and Mrs Mouse were getting closer and closer, mesmerised by his comforting voice and purring noise. Mrs Mouse said, 'Perhaps he's not such a bad chap after all. He seems interested in our house and everything.'

Clock could see what was happening and he needed to intervene somehow, but how was the question. His chime was switched off till tomorrow morning but this was an emergency. So with strain showing on his face he managed to do a very loud ting-a-ling which brought Mr and Mrs Mouse back to their senses and they withdrew to the back wall.

Cat looked up at Clock and made one of those spine chilling noises and scratched Clock's beautifully crested design on his base and spat and hissed and sloped off and as he went out of the door, he paused briefly and said, 'I'll be back.'

'That's the trouble with him,' claimed Clock. 'He looks at television a lot and he thinks he's Arnold Whatsanether and you'll never guess what they call him?'

CT said, 'What do they call him then?'

Clock said, 'I think it's a silly name, fancy calling him Stilton.'

'So that makes him the big Cheese around the house.' said CT not realising he had made a pun.

CT spread out his branches in despair 'What am I to do?'

Clock said, 'You keep asking that and I still can't give you an answer.'

Fairy who had fallen asleep for about a quarter of an hour awoke with a start. 'Gosh I needed that! What with standing on trees as a decoration and sometimes they just plonk you anywhere. The tree bits stick into the most delicate places and it is not nice. Some people just don't think of a fairy having delicate and private places.'

She took a deep breath and continued, 'What a day this has been, what with my tiara slipping and CT walking and mice to contend with and a very noisy Clock. It will be great to be placed back in my box.' Fairy took another deep breath and continued, 'It certainly wasn't like this last year, trees never used to be like this, they stood still and behaved themselves. What got into you, why did you think you could walk, there must be a reason?'

CT said, 'None whatsoever, I just thought it would be fun to do it.'

Fairy said quite suddenly. 'There's only one person who can tidy this room up and that is Father Christmas and he won't be here for another two and half hours so we must stay awake for his visit.'

Clock said, 'What are we going to do to pass the time?'

'Let's play I spy.' CT said.

Fairy said, 'How can we do that, I can't see a thing.'

Clock said, 'When CT thought he could walk and he slid across the floor, all the lights went out and the only light we had was the star on the end of your wand and now that's gone out.'

'I'm recharging it,' said Fairy.

Clock said, 'Where do you plug it in?'

'I don't plug it in anywhere – I place it under my arm for 30 minutes and then it's fully operational again.'

Clock, 'Is it ready yet?'

Fairy said, 'Yes!'

CT, 'Can you get my lights to light up again?'

Fairy said, 'I'll give it a try.'

Fairy closed her eyes and waved her wand in a large circle several times. At first there was a static sound, followed by a buzzing noise, then one by one the lights came on, which was rather clever because the lights were not plugged in.

CT said, 'You must have some powerful magic Fairy.'

'Well I do surprise myself now and again.'

The lights began to go out.

Fairy said, 'I'm not having any of this.' She flicked her wand upwards and they all came on again.

Fairy said, 'We have an hour of light, then we will be in the dark again until midnight.'

CT said, 'Can't we use your wand and star after the hour is up, I don't fancy being in the dark.'

'Okay,' Fairy said, 'I'll give it another charge.'

She placed the wand under her arm.

Clock said to Fairy, 'I have just noticed that your face is glowing.'

'Yes!' said Fairy, 'Every time I charge my star I glow a little.'

CT said, 'How long have we got to wait until midnight?'

'Well,' said Clock, 'Ten minutes ago we had two hours and twenty minutes.'

CT said, 'Are you going to tell me or not.'

Clock said, 'I just did, in plain language we have two hours and twenty minutes to wait.'

CT said, 'What we going to do to keep ourselves busy – we can't just do nothing?

Clock said, 'What do you suggest we do?'

Fairy said, 'Will you two stop nattering – it takes an awful lot of concentration, this re-charging lark – I just need another fifteen minutes or so and we will be fully charged – so be quiet!

Clock shut his eyes.

Fairy said, 'I didn't mean you could go to sleep.'

Clock said, 'I'm just resting my eyes.'

CT started singing Christmas Carols and his branches started to twitch.

Fairy said, 'I don't mind you singing but what is it with you, why are you twitching?'

CT said, 'It's getting cold in here.'

Clock said, 'Surely trees don't feel the cold – they are out in all sorts of weather!'

CT said, 'I was never out in cold weather, when it got below a certain temperature I was taken indoors.'

Clock said, 'Tell me you're joking?'

CT said, 'No of course not.'

'A bit mamby-pampy aren't we? Mummy's little boy get coldy-woldy then?' Fairy said, 'I wish you two would pack it in.'

Clock said, 'Well I ask you – if he hadn't tried to walk we'd be nice and warm in here because when he skidded across the floor he took out the plug of the electric fire.'

Fairy said, 'Alright! Alright! Don't keep on, what's done is done, okay?'

Clock said, 'Okay I'll keep quiet'

CT said, 'That will be a miracle.'

Fairy said, 'Don't you start, you are as bad as each other and I do need just another three or four minutes of quiet!'

Fairy said, 'There! That's it all done, I can now relax and I can see that the time is now ten o'clock, only two more hours to wait.'

CT said again, 'What are we going to do?'

'I know,' said Fairy, 'We'll do some breathing exercises.'

CT, 'What good will that do us?'

Fairy said, 'It will help to keep us warm.'

Clock said, 'What a silly idea.'

'Well,' said Fairy, 'If you can come up with a better idea, I'm listening.'

Nobody spoke.

Clock said, 'If you can make the lights come on – why not the fire?'

Fairy said, 'I can only work on amps – not kilowatts. Besides it's dangerous to leave a fire on all night.'

Clock said, 'Well it was going to stay on till midnight anyway.'

Fairy said, 'How do you know that?'

Clock said, 'The Master of the house wound me up today and he said straight into my face that he had set the timer to cut out for the fire and lights at midnight, because he knew that the temperature was going to drop tonight.'

CT said, 'I told you it was cold in here.'

Fairy said, 'You both will have to put up with it, we are all in the same boat.'

Both Clock and CT decided to risk going to sleep and they both shut their eyes. CT's breathing was laboured and Clock snored loudly. It was like living through a thunderstorm and Fairy who was feeling tired herself despite the noise dropped off to sleep.

Meow. Meow. RRRRRRROOOOWWW! Everyone woke up – it was dark and that meant it had gone past ten thirty – but how far past ten thirty was anybody's guess, fairy was fumbling with her wand and star trying to re-activate it and eventually she was able to get it working and she lifted it above her head and saw that the time was ten past eleven and then she lowered her wand and saw that Stilton the cat was standing in front of the mouse hole washing his paws. He flicked open the points just like a penknife and stretched and flared out his paws ready for action – he turned, made for the base of CT in commando style and jumped on the tub. His intention was to climb the tree and get the Fairy, not realising of course that all fairies could fly. There was a lot of groaning and rustling of branches, but CT was much more prickly than he first thought. He couldn't climb Clock, because he was too smooth. In the end he gave up and so he decided to make an assault on Mr & Mrs Mouse's home.

Clock whispered to both Fairy and CT, 'We got to get rid of Stilton before midnight.'

Fairy said, 'We know! Have you any practical suggestions?

Clock said, 'None.'

At this point in time we get closer to the floor where Stilton the cat is thinking of inviting two guests to a mouse supper. Stilton pushes himself right up to the skirting board and places his eye over the hole. All the lights are on, but there's no one in. Stilton frowns and moves away from the hole, 'I wonder where they are? They could be on a "cheese run" but which way did they go, behind the walls, back around the alley ways and under the floorboards or across the room and out through the door?' Stilton hadn't realised that he was speaking his thoughts out loud.

Clock said, 'Blooming heck. What's going to happen now?'

CT said, 'What's that?'

Clock said, 'It's Mr & Mrs Mouse. They have gone off on a shopping spree.'

Fairy said, 'Well it being Christmas they probably need to get foodstuff for their larder, they'll be fine if they have gone round the back.'

Clock said, 'They haven't.'

Fairy said, 'How do you know?'

Clock said, 'I've just seen them come round the door.'

Mr & Mrs Mouse were laden with food, Mr Mouse had found an old sock and he must have filled it right up with food and he was having a difficult time pulling it along. It would have been impossible to go round the back ways. Mr & Mrs Mouse saw Stilton's back and stopped, there was nowhere to hide, they were in open territory and this looked like the end for them.

Mr Mouse said to Mrs Mouse, 'Go to the side skirting board behind the door and keep in the shadows and work your way round, he won't see you.'

Mrs Mouse said, 'What about you?'

Mr Mouse said, 'Don't worry about me – I'll get through somehow.'

Mr Mouse looked up at the Fairy and spreads his tiny hands out and shrugged his shoulders in despair.

Fairy said, 'I may be able to help him, after all he did give me back my star.' Clock said, 'Only after much persuasion.'

'I know all that.' said Fairy, 'But it is getting near Father Christmas time.'

Stilton heard a rustle of something behind and turned round and saw Mr Mouse with his bag of food and got into his commando crouch position and slowly crawled to where Mr Mouse was shaking with fear. Mr Mouse swallowed nervously. He could run, but he would have to leave the food behind, but he just stood watching Stilton getting closer and closer and Stilton's paws with his points out swept round in a pincer movement, only to have his quarry snatched away by Fairy's magic wand. Mr & Mrs Mouse complete with the sock full of goodies were safely in their home. Mr Mouse placed both hands over his heart to try and stop it from beating so quickly.

There was a lot of noise outside their home as Stilton went berserk, yelling his head off and running all round the room, tearing the parcels with his sharp claws – all of a sudden the light went on and the Master walked into the room.

'Oh dear what a mess – Stilton look what you have done – How did you get in here you naughty boy - I'll have to get up early and tidy everything before the children come down – out you go Stilton.' The Master took one more look around the room and quietly closed the door shut.

CT, Fairy and Clock sighed with relief. It was just in time – because they could hear noises coming from the roof – and all of a sudden he was in the room - Father Christmas! 'Well what's been going on here – looks like you have had a riot!'

Fairy told Father Christmas the whole story. Father Christmas said to CT 'I hope you have learned your lesson young fellow me lad and you are going to behave yourself over Christmas and the new year.'

Yes. said CT, 'I promise.'

'That's good enough for me,' said Father Christmas. He went back up the chimney and as he left a trail of pure white stars swirled around the room and everything that had been damaged and torn had turned back to the way it was earlier that evening.

At seven o'clock in the morning the Master came into the room, switched on the light and clasped his hand to his head and said, 'My goodness – why everything is alright – I must have dreamt it all.'

Stilton had followed his master into the room because he was rubbing against his legs and the master picked him up and said, 'Happy Christmas Stilton!'

CT, Fairy and Clock thought the same thing.

The End.

Printed in Great Britain
by Amazon